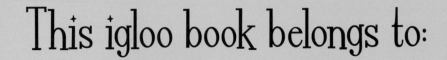
This igloo book belongs to:

. . . .

. . . .

igloobooks

Published in 2017
by Igloo Books Ltd
Cottage Farm
Sywell
NN6 0BJ
www.igloobooks.com

LEO002 0717
2 4 6 8 10 9 7 5 3 1
ISBN 978-1-78670-958-5

Written by David Styring
Illustrated by Jo Byatt
Song lyrics by Melanie Joyce

Designed by Kerri-Ann Hulme
Edited by Melanie Joyce

Narrated by Michael Ball
Music, song vocals and sound by Sam Park

Printed and manufactured in China

Catch Me If You Can!

David Styring

Jo Byatt

igloobooks

Once, there was a fish called Terence who was feeling very sad. He longed to swim just like his friends. He longed to impress his dad.

Ever since he could remember, Terence had only one wish,
To win the cup his dad had won and to be the fastest fish.

Terence was very determined.
He wanted to stand out.
He wanted to be good at swimming,
of that there was no doubt.

The problem for Terence was
that no matter how hard he tried,
Instead of swimming straight ahead,
he **wiggled** from side to side.

The last race that Terence had entered, his dad sat in the crowd.
"This is a brilliant chance," thought Terence,
"to make my dad so proud."

Terence darted off with a splash! He dived further than the rest...

... but instead of going forwards, he just wiggled east to west!

Soon, Terence was falling behind.
He had no chance of winning.
If Terence didn't speed up, he'd be back at the beginning!

Terence kept on swimming.
He wiggled his fins so fast.
He was sure he was going to win,
No thoughts of coming last.

Terence finally finished and listened for all the cheers.
He felt very upset indeed, when all he heard were jeers.

Dad swam over to Terence and said,
"Come on now, cheer up, son.
Don't take it all too seriously,
Swimming should be **fun**."

Something needed changing. It was plain for everyone to see.
Luckily, Dad had worked out what that simple change should be.
"You can do it, Terence," he said. "I know that you won't fail.
You just need to move your fins at the same time as your tail."

"When I was young," said Dad,
"I wasn't as fast as other fish.
Then I used my tail and fins together
and soon I got my wish."

So, Terence started practising, no matter what the weather.

Very soon his tail and fins worked perfectly together!

He listened to instruction, because he knew that Dad knew best.

Terence certainly put the work in.

His dad was SO impressed.

Discover four more fantastic picture books on audio CD...

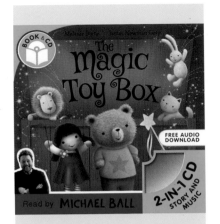

The clock has struck 12 and it's playtime for Lucy's adventurous toys. What will they get up to until morning? Enjoy this magical tale together at storytime.

Join Marvin and Maddie as they have fun playing tricks on all their jungle friends. This hilarious book is perfect for a shared storytime, full of laughter.

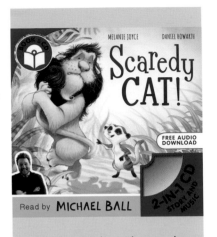

Lion is ready to leave the jungle, because he thinks he doesn't belong. Until, an unlikely little friend helps him believe in the power of friendship... and himself!

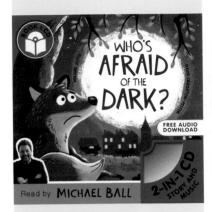

Little Fox is scared of creeping shadows and things that go bump in the night. But, with a little help from Mummy, he soon learns there's nothing to fear, after all.

Scan the QR code below for your free audio download!

or visit https://igloobooks.com/picturebookandcd

igloobooks